W9-COI-142

E
DeB

$9.52

De Bruyn, Monica
Lauren's secret ring

DATE DUE

OC 2 0 '90	NOV 9 '95	
JA23'9	JUL 2 5 '96	
FE 7'9	JUL 1 5 '97	
MR 7'91	OCT 2 1 '98	
AP 6'91	AP 0 5 '00	
JY22'9	NO 26 0	
OC 1'94	JY 1 6	
JY 1'9	OC 1 8	
1 6 '94	FE 0 9 '19	
1 '94	SE 1 6 20	

Lauren's Secret Ring

With thanks to Ann Fay and Kathleen Tucker
for their editorial assistance

Library of Congress Cataloging in Publication Data
De Bruyn, Monica
   Lauren's secret ring.

   (A Concept book)
   SUMMARY: Lauren learns that making and having
friends can be as magical and rewarding as the
fantasy life she builds around her secret ring.
   [1. Friendship — Fiction] I. Title.
PZ7.D3544 Lau   [E]   79-27261
ISBN 0-8075-4391-8

Text and Illustrations© 1980 by Monica De Bruyn
Published simultaneously in Canada by
General Publishing, Limited, Toronto
All rights reserved. Printed in U.S.A.

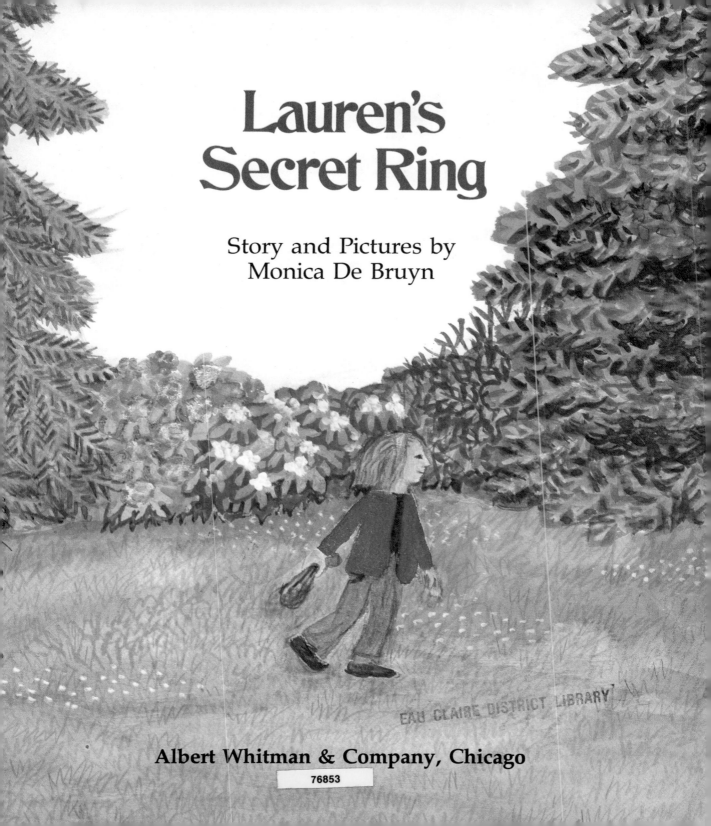

Lauren's Secret Ring

Story and Pictures by
Monica De Bruyn

EAU CLAIRE DISTRICT LIBRARY

Albert Whitman & Company, Chicago

76853

Lauren was new in town.
She didn't have any friends,
but she had a special secret.

She owned a magic ring.

She was feeding the ducks in
the park one day, when there
it was, shining on the ground.

"Maybe a little elf left it here
just for me," she thought as she
slipped the ring on her finger.

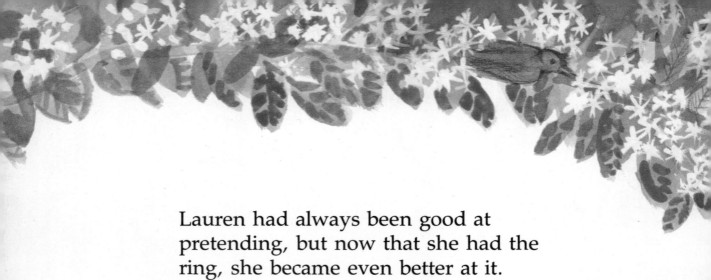

Lauren had always been good at
pretending, but now that she had the
ring, she became even better at it.

On her way home, she heard the birds
chirping in the trees. "I wonder what
they're singing about today," she said.

Lauren held the ring up and watched
it sparkle in the sunlight. Suddenly she
knew. The birds were talking about her!

"See! See! See!" chirped the sparrows.
"The ring! The ring!"

"She's got it! She's got it!" called
a bluejay.

A big old crow flew down beside
Lauren and almost grabbed the ring
with his beak.

"Aww, give it to me! Give it to me!"
he croaked. "I'll buy it from ya!"

"No!" said Lauren. "Not for all the
money in the world!"

In the morning, Lauren wore the ring to school.

She hated the long walk every day, with no one to talk to. "I wish I could fly," Lauren thought, turning the ring on her finger.

And suddenly, there she was, floating along as if she'd done it all her life!

Of course, only Lauren knew that as she entered the playground, her feet weren't *quite* touching the sidewalk.

After that, Lauren wore the ring
to school every day.

She didn't worry anymore about
knowing the right answers for her
new teacher. When she rubbed the ring,
she could think of just what to say.

EAU CLAIRE DISTRICT LIBRARY

And at recess, when the other
children played without Lauren,
she had her ring.

Sometimes she listened to the
birds talk.

Sometimes she would stop to see
Sharkey, the big dog that lived next
to school. By rubbing her ring, Lauren
could understand everything he said.

Sharkey was tired of sitting alone
in his tiny yard. With the help
of her ring, Lauren told him
beautiful stories.

Lauren's pets at home liked her to
rub the ring and tell stories, too.
She had five hamsters and was thinking
about getting a rabbit.

"I don't need any friends," Lauren
often thought. "I have my pets
and my ring."

Then one terrible day when Lauren awoke, her ring was gone!

She looked everywhere for it.

"Well, I just won't get up," Lauren decided, pulling the covers over her head. "I won't do anything today."

But Lauren's mother had a different idea. "It's time to get up, young lady!" she said. "You're not sick, and this is a school day."

Lauren dragged herself out of bed.

It took her a long time to get dressed that morning. And when she tried to eat her cereal, it seemed to stick in her throat.

Of course, without her ring, Lauren couldn't fly. It took forever to walk to school.

So Lauren was late!

All morning she sat very still.
What if the teacher called on her,
now that her ring was gone?

Suddenly the room was quiet.
"Lauren," her teacher was saying,
"I asked you what 6 plus 3 is."

Lauren jumped. "Oh, um . . ."
She paused. "Nine?"

Lauren's teacher smiled. "Very good."

Lauren didn't know how she had
gotten the right answer without her
ring. In a few minutes the noon bell
rang. She gave a sigh of relief.

Then she remembered.
She had left her lunch at home.

What an awful day!

Lauren sat down at the lunch table
and almost began to cry.

"What's wrong, Lauren?" asked a girl
named Sue.

"I forgot my lunch," Lauren said.

"Well, here, take this ham sandwich,"
Sue said. "I hate ham anyway."

Just then some other girls came by.

Julia gave Lauren an orange.
Mary gave her some cookies.
Cara gave her potato chips and cheese.
Lauren was so surprised. It felt like a party!

After lunch, Lauren took the girls
to meet Sharkey.

"Won't he bite?" asked Cara.

"Oh, no, he just wants a story,"
Lauren explained.

"Tell him a ghost story," said Sue,
"and see if he gets scared."

"Well, I'll try," Lauren said. But
she didn't know if she could,
without her ring.

She began a story about a haunted
doghouse. As she talked, Sharkey sat
perfectly still. Lauren could tell
this was the creepiest story she'd
ever made up.

Halfway through, the bell rang.

"Tell us the ending tomorrow,"
begged Julia.

"I will!" said Lauren.

After school, Lauren saw Sue again.

"Where do you live?" asked Sue.

"On Elm Street," said Lauren.

"Why, so do I! Come on over. My
brother caught a toad last night,
and we're building him a box."

When Lauren came home from Sue's
house, there was her ring on
the dining room table.

"I found that when I was cleaning,"
her mother said. "I thought it
might be yours."

Lauren just stared. Then she smiled.

She picked up her ring and tucked
it away in her jewelry box.

"I think I'll give it a rest for
a while," she said.

EAU CLAIRE DISTRICT LIBRARY